CU00865497

Text copyright © Michael Hardcastle 1999
Illustrations copyright © Chris Leishman 1999

First published in Great Britain in 1999
by Macdonald Young Books
an imprint of Wayland Publishers Ltd
61 Western Road
Hove
East Sussex
BN3 1JD

Find Macdonald Young Books on the internet at
http://www.myb.co.uk

The right of Michael Hardcastle to be identified as the author
and Chris Leishman as the illustrator of this Work has been
asserted by them in accordance with the Copyright,
Designs and Patents Act 1988

Designed by Leishman Design
Printed and bound by Guernsey Press

British Library Cataloguing in Publication Data available

ISBN: 0 7500 2794 0

Rivals United

MICHAEL HARDCASTLE

Illustrated by Chris Leishman

MACDONALD YOUNG BOOKS

Chapter One

Jake was jumping up and down on the spot because he was so upset. "Why can't you play?" he asked David. "I mean, we need you. Who'll score goals for us if you aren't in the team?"

"Look, I'm sorry, Jake, honestly. I wish I could play but I just can't."

"Is it to do with your dad?" Jake kept on. "Is it one of those Army secrets?"

David frowned and rubbed his cheek. "I don't know what you're talking about. Look, I've got to go, Jake. See you later. Oh, and I hope you win on Sunday."

Jake had calmed down by the time he reached Harry's house, though he was still thinking only about Sunday's match – the match of the season – the derby match between Roos East End and Roos West End. It was the match nobody dare lose otherwise life in the village would be unbearable.

So each team desperately needed its star players. And it was a fact that East End's most brilliant player was David Darley. He scored goals that made people blink and say, "Hey, that was really special, wasn't it?" He also created goals for others and, above all, he never gave up. Even if East End were two goals down with five minutes to go, David still believed they could win and would carry on playing his heart out.

Harry, the skipper of East End, was doing
homework on his computer when Jake arrived.
When she answered the door, his Mum sounded
as though she didn't want him interrupted, but
Jake said that he needed to see Harry urgently.

Harry really did seem to be gripped by what
he was doing. He was sitting on his bedroom
floor in front of the screen and didn't even look
up when Jake walked in. He kept running his
hand through his curly blond hair, something
he did when his team was having a bad time.

Suddenly though, he grinned, snapped, "Got it!" and set his fingers dancing over the keyboard. But Jake hardly noticed. There was only one topic on his mind.

"Did you know David won't be playing for us on Sunday?" he burst out. "That's terrible, isn't it, Harry?"

Harry nodded. "Yes. But I've just heard something much worse that that."

"Worse? There can't be anything worse than losing our best player for the most important match of the season," replied Jake, who took his football very seriously indeed.

"Well, how about David playing for West End and against us?" asked Harry, his grey eyes now focused on Jake waiting to see his reaction.

Jake didn't let him down. His face filled with horror. "What! That's crazy! David wouldn't play for them. He'd never want to play against his best mates! Harry, that's a mad idea. Where'd you get it from?!"

"From a friend. I'm not telling you who, but he plays for West End so he knows what he's talking about. David is definitely in their team for Sunday's match. That makes me really mad."

For once Jake was speechless.

Chapter Two

David was sitting on the sofa reading a football magazine when his father walked in. David looked up and immediately jumped to his feet, saluted and grinned.

"Is that your best uniform, Dad?" he asked. "There wasn't a special parade or something today, was there?"

His father smiled and brushed some imaginary dust from a badge on the khaki sleeve. "The answers are 'no' and 'yes', but I'm impressed you think my second best is in perfect shape."

"Any news of the move yet, Dad?"

"I've heard nothing," said Major Darley, turning on the TV and sinking into an armchair. "Maybe teletext knows more about the Army's plans than I do. Let's have a look.

Before either of them could read a word, the phone rang. David dashed to answer it. "Hello," he said.

"Traitor!" was the only word spoken by the caller.

"What?" David gasped. But the other person had hung up.

"Wrong number?" enquired his father, without looking up.

"Er, I think so," David replied, feeling his cheeks turn red.

A couple of minutes later, the phone rang again. David snatched it up. "Yes?" he said this time.

"If you play for West End on Sunday, you'll wish you hadn't," a voice threatened. Then the phone clicked into silence.

"Another one?" Major Darley asked, eyebrows raised.

"Must be," muttered David, who thought he recognized the caller. It wasn't the same person who'd rung earlier.

"Well, if it goes again don't bother to answer it," the Major recommended.

"I definitely won't," David assured him.

David took a ball into the garden and started some training exercises. He flicked the ball up from one foot to another, then from toe to thigh, before allowing it to bounce again. Sometimes, he tried to improve his record of how long he could keep the ball on the go, without allowing it to touch the ground. Now, though, he knew there'd be no new record today. He simply couldn't concentrate. His mind was fixed on other things.

Chapter Three

That night, David found it impossible to drop off to sleep. He couldn't stop worrying about the derby match and the part he intended to play in it. Was he doing the right thing in playing for West End? Would he fit in with their style of play? Most important of all, would his East End team-mates ever forgive him?

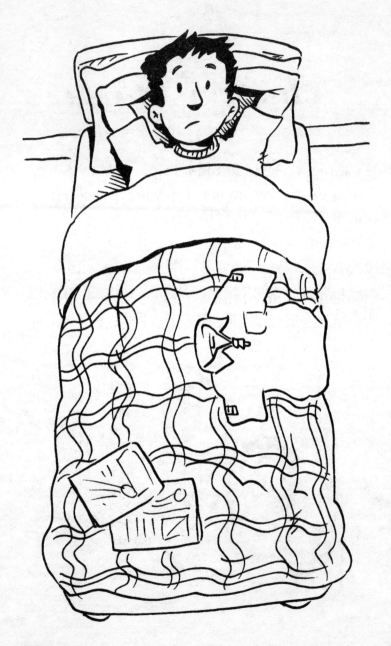

But when they knew the reason he was changing sides, surely they'd understand that he had no choice. On the other hand, those hostile phone calls showed how angry some people were.

David was sure the second call was from Sam, a mid-fielder with West End. He'd recognized his voice. On Sunday they'd be team-mates, so why didn't Sam want him to play? Unless, it suddenly occurred to David, Sam was afraid that David might take his place in the team. Jealousy, in other words. Yes, he nodded to himself, that could be it.

In spite of solving that little puzzle, David still couldn't get to sleep. He started to think about the friends he'd be letting down by playing for the opposition. In particular, he worried about Jake who, he realized, really looked up to him. So what would it be like when they both turned up for training on Tuesday evening?

On Tuesday, however, David didn't kick
a ball or say a word to Jake. The coach,
James Dore, wouldn't allow him to take any
part in the training session.

Then he took him to one side and asked,
in a voice as frosty as the weather, "Is it true
you're playing for West End on Sunday?"

David nodded.

"Then why did you think you'd be welcome here? Unless, of course, you've decided to come along and tell us what everyone else in the town seems to know already. Just what are you playing at, David?"

"I'm really sorry but I can't say," he tried to explain. "Not yet. But, I know what I'm doing."

"That's not good enough," the coach replied sharply. "West End want our best player and you're disloyal enough to accept whatever they're offering! Maybe they've asked you to be their skipper. I know you wanted to be captain before I picked Harry. No, don't interrupt – I don't want to hear any more lies. I don't want you talking to any of our players. Just go!"

David had no option. He cast a last glance at his team-mates and then, without another word, he set off home through the lightly falling snow.

Chapter Four

On the night before the derby match David received another phone call. "Who is it?" he asked suspiciously as his dad held out the receiver.

"He says he's a friend of yours," said David's dad. David took the phone hoping it was news about whether the county selector was going to attend the Roos derby. When he recognized Jake's voice, his heart slowed down.

"Listen, I know I'm not supposed to be talking to you," Jake began, his words rushing like a waterfall. "But I've got to know – why are you doing it?"

"Doing what?" David replied, innocently.

"You know what I mean – playing for the enemy, West End."

"Jake, I told you before. It's a secret. You can't tell secrets to anyone."

"Don't talk rubbish," said Jake. "You just don't want to tell me. And I thought we were friends."

David seized on that remark. "We are friends, but I can't tell anyone about this. Not even you."

There was silence at the other end of the line and David guessed Jake was going to put the phone down. Then Jake said, "Well, I'll tell you a secret for nothing. Lots of soldiers and their wives are ordering foreign money at the bank. So that means the Army are on the move, my mum says. And she works at the bank, so she must know."

"Oh, right," said David, suddenly interested. "Which country are they going to?"

"Not telling you!" Jake shouted. "If you won't share your secret, I'm not telling you mine. So we'll just see what happens on Sunday when we play your new team."

"OK," David replied, more calmly than he felt. "But I hope East End win, Jake. I mean that, honestly. Even though I'll be playing for West End."

Jake was so surprised by that remark he didn't know what to say. What did David mean? It didn't make sense.

Chapter Five

Next morning, David was eating breakfast when the phone rang. Was this another angry call about his loyalty, or even a threat about the match that was kicking off in less than two hours? This time, however, his dad picked up the receiver and got deep in conversation about Army matters. David sighed with relief. Then he overheard something about 'moving next week' and found himself listening to his dad's replies. The long-awaited news about future plans must have broken.

His dad's smile was as bright as sunrise when he put the phone down. "We're staying! I've got a promotion and a new job at Roos Camp. Your mum will be so pleased! And it means you can carry on playing football here."

"But what about Jake and Harry and their families? Are they staying as well? I mean, you thought they were definitely going to move abroad." His mouth was suddenly dry because, if they were now staying, then he'd have to change his plans. In fact, all his careful planning would have been wasted because he would prefer to play for East End rather than West.

Major Darley's smile had faded and he was shaking his head. "Sorry, David, but I'm afraid you're going to lose your best pals. Those families and many of the others who are in quarters at East Roos are pulling out. Looks like the East End football team will have to recruit some new players from somewhere. Still, new families will be posted in to Roos Camp before long, I expect."

By now David's mind was in a whirl. There were just so many things to think about. But he needed to know one thing right away. "Will everyone know about this today, before the big match begins, I mean?"

"Doubt it. Some people know, but I don't think its been posted up for everyone to see yet."

"Oh," said David. When his old team mates at East End found out that half of their players were leaving town, they were going to be even more angry with David for deserting them...

Chapter Six

Jack, the towering captain of West End, greeted his new team-mate with a very public hand-shake. "This is the hand of friendship," he declared, squeezing hard. "We used to be enemies. Now we're going to be the best of friends and you're going to score brilliant goals so that we can beat your old team out of sight."

David, aware that some East End players were watching, winced as he took his hand back and tried to smile. It would have been easier for him if they'd jeered or said something. Instead they just stared at him sullenly. David was convinced they would get their own back on him during the game. He'd have to play his very best to outwit them.

"Listen," Jack said to David, "I know we've not been good enough to get into the League. But with you in our team I reckon we can do it. That's why we wanted you. That's why you wanted to join us, isn't it?"

"Yeah," agreed David, knowing that wasn't quite the truth. He didn't think it would help to tell Jack about the departure of so many Roos East families.

After the recent hard frosts, the village-green pitch was rock-hard and all the players knew there was a risk of injury on such a surface. David stripped off his tracksuit. It felt strange to him to be wearing the red and white colours of West End instead of the blue and yellow of his old team. Several spectators were already gathering at the side of the pitch and David glanced over to see whether he could spot the person who might change his life.

One of the coaches at the leisure centre had told David that Tom Emley was planning to attend the next Roos derby on the lookout for young players. He'd seen Tom Emley only once, but had never forgotten him. How could any ambitious player forget the top county coach and selector?

So far, though, there was no sign of the stocky figure with the deep set eyes and dark beard. Maybe, he didn't always turn up for the whole match. In any case, he might be on the far side of the pitch where the morning mist still hung in the air.

As the teams lined up, David caught Jake's eye and didn't know whether to smile. But Jake was looking very glum so David just raised an eyebrow at him. He got no response.

Will, who was playing behind David, was just as ambitious as him. As captain of the Bazby School team he was also used to telling other players what to do. "Get going, Dave, soon as you can," he called. "Let's get one in the net against this lot before they know what's hit 'em."

His voice carried right across the pitch. Every East-Ender must have heard him. That would definitely help to raise the temperature.

David was sure of one thing – this was a game he'd never forget.

Chapter Seven

Within a minute of the start, a shoulder charge had sent David tumbling when he'd already parted with the ball. The ref hadn't seen, so the offender got away with it. David rubbed at the graze on his knee, picked himself up and ran to join in an attack. Even though his knee was painful he wouldn't let anyone know he was hurt.

It was minutes before he next had the ball. East End launched attack after attack, inspired from midfield by Jake who simply couldn't put a foot wrong. Even so they couldn't get the ball in the net. Harry came closest with a fierce drive from the edge of the box which flew wide of the upright. By the time David won possession in a skirmish, the pain in his knee had gone.

Moments later, he was hardly into his stride when he spotted that East End's keeper was well off his line. With wonderful judgement of speed and distance, David didn't even pause before shooting the ball high over the stranded keeper and into the back of the net. It was the best chipped shot he'd ever achieved and the first goal of the match!

David couldn't help feeling a sense of guilt at scoring against his old team-mates but he knew it happened all the time in professional football when players had been sold to a new club. As he turned to celebrate with other West-Enders, he spotted Tom Emley standing right on the touchline. And the selector was applauding as enthusiastically as any of the team's fans.

Harry was running his fingers through his curly blond hair. He was obviously annoyed. But there wasn't time to think about loyalties because West End had launched another attack, with Will keen to play the striker. Will exchanged passes with Sam Vickers, another midfielder with a talent for scoring spectacular goals. But Will blasted his shot high over the bar when he thought he was within range of the net.

Just before half-time, David was brought
down by a tackle from behind as he attempted
to get into the box. As he got to his feet he saw
that the offender was Harry, now being given
a lecture by the ref, who was already holding up
a yellow card. "Well, he's a traitor!" David heard
his former skipper mutter.

The ref frowned. "Don't know what you're
trying to say, lad. He's a player and he's got to be
protected. You commit another offence like that,
and it'll be your last on this pitch. Understand?"

Harry pushed his fingers through his hair again and muttered, "yes".

As half-time approached, all the players noticed that more and more spectators were arriving. Most of them were their own families.

Suddenly, there was a loud call from one mum. "Come on, you East-Enders! If this is your last game, make sure you win it. Let's leave on a victory note!"

It was just as well the ref blew for half-time, then because some of the boys in blue and yellow were open-mouthed with surprise. David watched as the team went into a huddle with James Dore, their coach, and guessed they'd be getting details of the Army's plans.

David wished he could go across and hear who was staying and who was leaving. He'd been in their team for so long it felt weird to be apart from them, and even worse to be wearing West End's colours. He hated being labelled a traitor. But he'd made his own move and he couldn't change now. He had done it knowing that the East End families would be leaving. If East End was disbanded, there'd be a rush for players to join West End. He'd had to make sure that there was a place for him on the team. He just couldn't ruin his chances of becoming a professional football player.

David was only half-listening to the West End coach. He was telling the team to keep up its attacking momentum in the second half when Tom Emley appeared and stood next to David.

"You're having a good game, son," the selector told him. David was surprised, he hadn't expected to be spoken to during a match. "And you made the right move. You and West End fit with each other like a hand in a glove. They'll need you all the more when they lose Will and Sam."

David stared. "Is the Army moving their families, too? I thought just the East End team would be affected."

Tom Emley was shaking his head. "This move's bigger than anyone thought. It involves lots of families, civilian as well as Army. That's why I'm here, to see whether we can patch together one team out of what's left. You see, we could do with a lively new team in the League. The East End and West End sides have never been quite good enough as separate units in the past."

"So you're not here today to pick players for a county match then?" asked David, still feeling bewildered.

"Not today. Maybe later, when the new team gets its act together. No, David, today I'm just doing what the Army asked me to do – to see if we can find a way of making up for so many departures. Anyway, you'd better get back on the pitch, son. The ref's ready to start the second half. Keep going forward. That's where your talent lies."

As he ran to take up his position, all David could think about was that his planning and scheming had been almost a waste of time. If there was going to be only one team from now on, it was a certainty he'd play. But at least now the county selector had seen him in action and would remember him for the future.

At the first break in the game, while an injury was being treated, David spoke to Jake. "Are your family going, Jake?" he asked.

To his surprise, Jake shook his head. "Oh, then we'll be team-mates again soon," David told him.

Jake looked amazed. "How d'you mean?"

"Can't tell you yet, but trust me, Jake," David said hurriedly before the game restarted. As he darted forward to pick up a pass, he was sure he saw Jake begin to smile.

Chapter Eight

As if they all knew this was to be their last match, the East-Enders pulled together and fought like tigers to grab the equalizer. David followed Jack's instructions to drop deeper and deeper into defence, until he was playing like an extra full-back. There was only about a minute remaining when East End won a free kick, right on the edge of the West End penalty area. David took up a position at the end of the defensive wall organized by Jack.

The players already knew that Harry had a very strong kick. So the defenders ducked as Harry blasted the ball towards them. It cannoned off one player and, when David stuck out a foot to push the ball to safety, the spin caused it to loop away. It spun up and over the goalkeeper's despairing attempt at a catch – and into the back of the net.

Roos West End 1, Roos East End 1.

It was obviously an own goal, but Harry claimed it for himself. The East-Enders were all cheering. David couldn't believe what he'd done. He thought he should apologize to somebody but then he couldn't see who would listen. His West End team-mates might even think he'd scored it on purpose. But, if this was to be the very last West End v East End game, perhaps it was only right that the only boy who'd ever played for both teams should score for each of them.

When, moments later, the ref blew the whistle for full-time, the players dutifully shook hands with their opponents and David found Jake smiling at him. "Well, we didn't win like you hoped we would. But you did your best for us. Thanks, David."

David just grinned because there was nothing he could say.

The last word came from Tom Emley. "Funny way to finish a game, David, but that's the way it goes sometimes. You could always say you were playing for the future of both teams. Just make sure you score in the right net next time."

A few days later, after the soldiers and their families left, a new team was formed from the remaining players of East End and West End. It was called, of course, Roos United.

Read more of Michael Hardcastle's soccer stories:

SOCCER SECRET
Tom is a brilliant striker and he likes nothing better than
boasting about all the goals he scores.
What he doesn't know is that his cousin, Alan,
is good at football too – as a goalie.
When will Alan get the recognition he deserves,
without upsetting Tom?

INJURY TIME
Joe would be a really good player, if he weren't so
accident-prone. He always seems to be suffering
from aches and pains and rarely gets
through a match without injury.
The coach thinks that he's a fake, but Amy's not sure.
Could there be another reason for Joe's problem?

STRIKER'S BOOTS
Sean has waited for weeks to get a place in the school
soccer team. He's almost given up hope when the coach
picks him at last! Then disaster strikes. He's forgotten
his boots. How can he play? This could be his big chance,
but how on earth can he score goals in bare feet?

For more information about Mega Stars,
please contact: The Sales Department,
Macdonald Young Books,
61 Western Road, Hove,
East Sussex BN3 1JD